Lizzie Dripping and the Little Angel

Helen Cresswell

illustrated by
Faith Jaques

*For Anna, Angela and Paul
with love and thanks*

Published by BBC Books,
A division of BBC Enterprises Ltd
Woodlands, 80 Wood Lane, London W12 0TT

First published 1974
New edition 1990
© Helen Cresswell 1974

ISBN 0 563 12688 4

Typeset in Times by
Ace Filmsetting Ltd, Frome, Somerset

Cover printed by Richard Clay Ltd, Norwich
Printed and bound in Great Britain by Richard Clay Ltd, Bungay

Contents

Lizzie Dripping
and a Birthday Wish

The Arbuckles looked at the cake. Lizzie had just pressed in the last fruit jelly to make the pattern complete. The whole cake was covered in sweets—"A rainbow cake," Lizzie thought.

"Well, I don't know," said Patty at last. "Not usual run o' birthday cakes *this* ain't."

"But I *wanted* it to be unusual!" cried Lizzie. "*Gramma's* unusual!"

"Aye. And *that* depends how you look at it," Patty said.

"It's a right pretty cake, our Lizzie," said Albert. "Good enough to eat, that looks. Try one, can I?"

He stretched out a hand and Lizzie squealed and Patty gave his hand a slap.

"Like a two-year-old!" she said. "Come to that, *cake* for a two-year-old, that looks, never mind seventy. If you'd stuck it over with mint imperials, mind. . . ."

"Well, I like it, and I reckon Gram will," said Lizzie. "Cake and sweets all rolled in one. I think them sweets stuck on is the best part."

"Come on then," said Patty, "clear it out the way. She'll be walking in that door under an hour, and nose like a blood-hound for anything she's not meant to know."

"Time for dinner, I reckon," Albert put in. "Peckish, looking at that."

"Only pity is about *candles*," said Lizzie hopefully.

"Now don't you set on about that again," Patty told her. "You get past twenty-one, you don't *have* candles. There's only you'd *think* of seventy candles, Lizzie Dripping."

Patty went to fetch a tin and Lizzie went on staring at the multi-coloured cake, but what she was seeing was a cake that *did* have seventy candles, each with a tiny pointed tip of flame, and—

"Mam!" she cried. Patty turned. "Just *seven* candles, Mam! Just something for her to blow out and make a wish."

"Aye, that'd do," agreed Albert.

Patty hesitated.

"*Please*, Mam! Might never have a birthday at our house again, Gram, mightn't."

"Not that many more, here or anywhere," Patty said.

Lizzie stared. "What d'ye mean?"

"Oh, do stop plaguing, Lizzie!" cried Patty. "And get cleared up, quick!"

Lizzie did not move. She looked at Albert, and he moved his pipe from one side of his mouth to the other.

"Getting old, your Gramma is," he explained. "That's all your mother meant."

Lizzie turned away.

"Go on, then!" she heard Patty's voice. ""Here's candles, and you'll find holders, if you have a rummage. Look sharp now!"

"Oh, thank you, Mam!"

And so Lizzie was saved from thinking what she *had* been going to think, and began instead to find candle holders, pink and blue and yellow. Even so, it was not long before she started to think again.

"Do people have to get old?" she wondered. "All of them, whether they want to or not? *I* don't want to get old. That witch, *she's* old . . . bet she's hundreds of years old! Hundreds and hundreds. Wonder if . . . what if I could go and see . . . ? She might—I mean, *'tis* Gram's birthday. What if she'd let Gram have a wish, a real wish, that'd come true? Always ask. . . ."

Lizzie nodded to herself, and put in the candles, each in a holder like a flower, making a garden that would light up later,

when the time came, more like stars than flowers.

An hour later Lizzie Dripping was waiting at the bus stop at Bilbury with such impatience that she began to feel sure the bus would never come. Her eyes positively ached with looking, so she looked away from the road and at the pit head instead, right nearby. Just then the pit siren let out its long, lonely wail, and although she had heard it a thousand times before, and although it was broad daylight and the sun shining, Lizzie gave a little shiver.

She stared at the familiar outline of the pit head, at the wheels and towers, and thought of the men down there in the dark, and though she tried hard *not* to think it, thought, "There's men down there. Miners. Right under my feet this very minute, could be." She stared down at the ground by her feet as if by staring hard enough and long enough she could actually be able to see down there.

"My Grampa died down there. Killed in a roof fall, before ever I was born. Six men, all killed. . . . Wonder what my Grampa was like? Mam says he was the salt of the earth—what's *that* mean, I wonder . . . ?"

Lizzie looked deliberately away again and stared expectantly at the bend in the road round which the bus would appear. After a minute or two she again began to have that queer, nightmarish feeling that it never *would* come.

"Like a watched kettle," she thought. "Watched kettle never boils, watched bus never comes."

So Lizzie shut her eyes. When she did not hear the approach of the bus straight away, she took further steps.

"It'll come by the time I've counted fifty," she told herself. Eyes still shut, she began counting, and had only reached eight when she heard the throb of an engine. The magic had worked.

Lizzie danced up and down as it drew up. A case and two black bags were handed down and Gramma herself at last appeared and climbed squarely and carefully down.

"Gramma!" cried Lizzie, and threw her arms about her and felt the soft, dry, papery skin, and smelt the familiar smell of eau-de-cologne and mints. (Gramma got through a bag of mint imperials every day. "Got no teeth left to rot, and good for the digestion," was what she said.)

"Hello, my little duck!" she said.

"Happy Birthday, Gram! I've got a present for you, but not till teatime, Mam says."

"Let's have a look at you." Gramma pushed her to arm's length and looked at her. "You've growed again, Lizzie, I swear you have."

Lizzie was nearly as tall as Gramma now. She often wondered that so small a body as Gramma should have produced a daughter as big as Patty.

"Near as tall as you, I am," she said.

Gramma looked round. "Where's Albert?"

"Oh, Dad's coming," Lizzie assured her. "Said we could start walking if things weren't too heavy, or else wait here. He's just gone to the shop in Bilbury for some things for the garden."

"You don't come to stop away without a bit of luggage," said Gramma.

"Oh I know. He'll not be long. Let's feel." Lizzie picked up a case and smiled. " 'S all right. I can carry this a bit. Start walking, shall we?"

Gramma nodded, straightened her hat and picked up a bulging bag in each hand. They set off, and soon had rounded the corner and were walking with the colliery tip rearing above them on their right hand like a black, conical mountain. Lizzie saw Gramma look at it out of the corner of her eye, and thought, "Poor Gramma. Must hate looking at that tip. Mam says she thinks of Grampa every time she sees it. Better say something— take her mind off it."

"Last day at school today, Gram," she told her. "I've not been at all this morning, stopped at home to help Mam with—well, to help Mam. And we've only to go back for an hour after dinner, Miss Platt says, and then we can come home early."

"That's nice," said Gramma absently. She was still thinking about Grampa, Lizzie could see that.

"And you know what—we might go to the *sea* for a day while you're here. Mam said so. Wouldn't it be smashing?"

Gramma did look interested now.

"Aye, well, that would be nice. Do with a good breath of the sea. Give me lungs a good clear out. Cough cough cough all winter I've been. Oooh—here's Albert now!"

The van drew up and Albert got out, beaming. He liked Gramma, Lizzie knew that. Next minute they were bundled into the van, luggage and all, and being driven merrily towards Little Hemlock, home, and dinner.

The school bell rang for the last time that term, and only seconds later Lizzie Dripping was out and away in the hot sun, walking home.

"All the time I want now," she thought. "All the time in the world . . ."

And it was as if she were walking into the wide world because beyond the roofs of Little Hemlock were the hills, wave upon wave of them. Lizzie knew full well that when you reached them they were just hills like any others—springy turf, daisies, scent of clover. But now they were made mysterious by distance and even looked faintly blue, though certainly they must be green.

Lizzie remembered the witch again. *She* had become more mysterious by distance. She had always been mysterious, of course, but now that Lizzie had not seen her for nearly a whole month she herself had become a little hazy, as the hills were. and beckoning. And more than a little fearful . . .

"But I *shall* see her again soon," she thought. "Oh witch—I'm coming!"

It was not just any witch Lizzie was thinking about, but *her* witch.

"I can do without the others," she thought.

She still had not forgotten that day in Little Hemlock grave-yard when all at once there had been three witches, hunched like ravens on the tomb of Hannah and Cyril Post (*Peace Perfect Peace*) all looking at her, and all a-twitch with spells.

"Just my witch," she thought. "She's different. Could've changed, mind. Never really know where you are, not with that witch."

She walked on, seeing blue hills and beckoning witches, then all at once stopped dead.

"Could've gone!" she cried out loud. "Oh no—not *gone*!"

Black and white Patch, above her on the edge of the Stokes's garden wall, started to bark and dance among the roses, and she began to run.

"I'll go and look, minute I've been home. Oooh—she must be there! I want to ask her about that wish!"

She ran then, all the way home. And as she went up the worn hollow steps to the garden there was Toby sitting in the border, and there was Gramma in a chair by the hollyhocks, dozing. She wore the felt hat she always wore "to keep sun off" and her old hands were folded peacefully in her lap and the bees made

8

paths in the air and hummed about her and Lizzie smiled a little to herself.

"Old she is, Gramma," she thought, and stood looking at her, the witch quite forgotten.

"*I'll* be old one day.' She spread her own hands and looked down at them, then back again to Gramma's which were soft and loosely veined and floury looking, almost.

"Mam first, though,' she thought. "She'll be old before I am."

Even that was hard to imagine. Lizzie shut her eyes and tried hard to see Patty with white hair dozing in a chair in the sun. It did not work. She could not even get so far as seeing Patty's hands folded in her lap, doing nothing.

"You've done, then."

Lizzie opened her eyes and was startled to see Gramma's open too, and looking at her.

"Oooh yes, Gramma. It's holidays now!"

"You'll not get far in life with your eyes shut," remarked Gramma. She picked up a sock she had been darning from a basket by her chair, and popped in a mint imperial from the bag in her pinafore pocket.

"I was only shutting 'em for a *minute*," protested Lizzie. "While I thought about something, see."

"Aye, well," said Gramma, "I do a fair deal of that myself, I s'pose, these days. Eyes shut, thinking on things, dreaming . . ."

"What d'you think *about*, Gramma?" asked Lizzie, all of a sudden curious and surprised to think that an old woman could sit dreaming. She dropped to the warm grass beside her. "What were you thinking about now—just then, when I came up?"

"Oooh—lot of old nonsense."

"Go on, Gram, tell me. You weren't asleep, were you?"

The old black-laced shoes came together as if to attention and Gramma was sitting bolt upright now.

"Go to sleep?" she cried. "Of a daytime? Me? You'll not catch *me* asleep of a daytime, my girl. Bed—that's the place for sleeping. Never been any lying about in *my* family. My old mother,

9

you know how old she was when she died?"

"Eighty-four?" said Lizzie, who knew.

"All of eighty-four year old. And never a nap in all her born days. 'Plenty of time for that when you're up there!'—that's what she'd say to me." And Gramma jerked her head.

"When you're—where, Gramma?" Lizzie asked, half guessing, half not even wanting to know.

"There! Up in the churchyard, under a stone. Plenty of time then for sleeping in the daytime. 'Day and night and for ever and ever till kingdom come'—that's what she used to say, and I've not forgot it. Never."

"She means it," thought Lizzie wonderingly. "You can tell she does. But she *was* asleep just now, I know she was. And I've seen her napping before, plenty of times. Funny . . . but you can't call her a fibber . . . she thinks it's true. It's only fibbing if you say a thing and you *know* it isn't true. . . ."

Lizzie heard the cuckoo far away down by the beeches.

"They call *me* a fibber, though," she thought, "and *that* isn't fair, neither. And if I was to tell them about my witch . . . !"

She sat up suddenly. The witch! Clean forgotten in that hot summer stillness held between the high hedges and the old red brick of the cottage walls.

"That you, Lizzie?" Patty's voice came through the open door.

"Yes, Mam!"

"Toby all right, is he?"

"Yes, Mam." Lizzie sighed, then got up and picked up her satchel. She went into the living-room and instead of the dim coolness she had expected, was met by air hotter than ever.

"Phew!" she gasped. "Hot in here! Hello, Mam."

She had only a cloud of steam as answer to her greeting.

"There's only me daft enough to start off ironing and baking all at one go on a day like this." Patty's hair fell damply over her face. "Birthday today, anniversary supper tomorrow. . . . Oh, I could die of it, I swear I could! Put the kettle on, Lizzie, will you, for a cup of tea. If I don't sit down soon, I shall—ooooh!"

She let out a shriek, banged down the iron and pushed past Lizzie into the scullery. There she opened the oven, snatched out a tray of tarts, faintly steaming, and dropped them onto the ironing board.

"And *now* look! Done brown and dry as biscuits and meant to be sponge! *Them* ain't going to any anniversary supper. Not having 'em say *I* don't know how to cook a bakewell. *We* shall have to eat them, for our teas, and—"

"Now what? Now what's up?"

It was Gramma, peering in at the door and sniffing.

"Nothing, Ma,' said Patty in a voice that said exactly the opposite. "You get back out and finish your nap. Just a few bakewells done a bit over, that's all."

" 'Tain't bakewells *I* smell,' said Gramma, advancing a little. Then it was her turn to shriek. "Your iron, girl!"

Patty screamed again and dived out to lift the iron. Beneath it was a towel, faintly smoking and imprinted with an iron-

11

shaped brown pattern, rather like a shield.

"Oooh! Would you *believe*!"

"If I've told you once, Patty," said Gramma righteously, "I've told you a thousand times. One job at a time." She came right in now, and started to move about in a vague way as if looking for something, all the while muttering to herself under her breath. "I dunno . . . makes you wonder if you wasn't wasting your time. All them years, year in, year out, raising kids, and—I dunno . . . times I've told you . . ."

"Out of my way, Lizzie!" cried Patty then, interrupting the flow. "And pick that satchel off the floor, will you? You'll not be satisfied till I've broke my neck over your dropped things. Bad enough going round all day after that dratted baby—and where's he? Who's minding him?"

She threw the door wide, hoping, Lizzie knew, to catch out Gramma, who had been supposed to be minding him. There squatted Toby, right out of the storm, dropping stones into his bucket to hear them clang. Lizzie stared at him dejectedly.

"Gramma nagging at Mam, Mam nagging at me," she thought. "Nag nag nag. Wish *I* was Toby. Only one round here don't get nagged at, he is. Never think it was someone's *birthday* . . ."

"Now look," said Patty, "I shall go clear out of my mind if things don't get sorted out soon. And birthdays on top of all else, and tea to lay." Here she shot another look at Gramma, who was inspecting the damage to the towel and ironing board, and still clucking under her breath. "You get Toby in his chair, Lizzie, and give him a push round. That'll be two less under my feet."

"Yes," thought Lizzie, "go and see witch then, I can, and ask her. . . ."

"All right, Mam," she said out loud.

"And fetch me some mint imperials, shall you, Lizzie, from the shop," said Gramma. "A quarter, that'll do for now. And get 'em to weigh 'em out. I don't want any of them nasty plastic bags. Here's money.' Then she lowered her voice. "And here's a few pence for yourself."

"Thanks, Gram," Lizzie took the money and gave Gramma a conspiratorial smile.

She went outside and picked up Toby, who was very dirty, and plonked him into his pushchair.

"Come on, lump," she said. "Tatas."

Lizzie often called Toby "lump" to hide how much she loved him. And she loved him mainly because he so obviously and joyously loved her.

"And you be careful!" came Patty's voice after her. "You watch out for them lorries and keep on the pavement, where you can!"

And so Lizzie set off, first walking and then at last, feeling joy coming back in a flood, running.

"Holidays, anyhow!" she thought. "And birthday tea tonight!"

She ran between the high hedges and creamy sprays of hemlock, smelling the summer and seeing ahead the narrowed blue

13

sky, all at once certain again that the holiday would be a good one. The pushchair jumped and rattled over the stones and Toby gurgled.

"Going to see a witch, Toby," she told him.

She liked Toby because she could say anything at all to him, and still get a beam for answer. And he was only two—much too young to tell tales.

"He doesn't know what a witch is, even," she thought. "Oooh, she must be there, she must! Only thing is—what if Toby's scared, or what if he yells and frightens her off?"

Lizzie slowed her pace, pondering the problem. She could not decide whether Toby would frighten the witch, or vice versa, or both. Then she felt the coins that Gramma had given her sticky in her palm, and knew at once what the answer was.

"Come on, Toby," she cried. "Got to go up to the shop, any-how!"

Ten minutes later, hotter than ever now and out of breath, she was wheeling the pushchair into the shaded drive by the church porch.

"Here we are! Come on now, Toby, out you get!"

She lifted him up, took his hand, and Toby obediently followed her along the steep little path that led up by the church. When you started up the path all you could see ahead was the grass fringing the sky, and Lizzie thought of it as a path-way into the sky itself. Often she found herself curiously flat and disappointed to find she was at the top and still on earth, after all.

They reached the rusty iron gate that led into the churchyard itself. Lizzie stopped and listened. Her heart thudded right up in her throat.

She heard the comfortable croon of pigeons and stock-doves in the high trees, the drone of insects and a faint, never-ending whisper of leaves and grasses. She heard all the usual and familiar sounds of a summer day and yet knew in her heart of hearts that in itself that meant nothing at all. If the witch were

14

there, she would be *silently* there. She would be silently and invisibly there in the somehow greenish air of the graveyard under the yews, waiting for Lizzie alone to call her out into the world.

Lizzie drew in a deep breath and pushed open the gate.

"I must put Toby where he won't see the witch," she thought. "And her not see him, for that matter!"

Lizzie did not altogether trust the witch. She had offered once before to turn Toby into a toad, and was certainly capable of it if the fancy took her. She had turned the Briggs's cat into a toad with a mere crack of the knuckles, and had been quite tetchy about turning him back again. Lizzie looked about for a suitable tombstone as hiding place.

"That'll do," she decided, settling for *Abel Arthur Grey, Gone to Rest*, which was broad and high and not surrounded by grass and nettles as some of the others were. A stung Toby would certainly yell—witch or no witch.

15

"Come on, Toby, here," she said. She spoke in a whisper, though she had an uneasy feeling that if the witch were there (in whatever world of her own went on invisibly side by side with Lizzie's own) she would be able to see and hear every single thing that was going on.

"There's a good boy. Now there you are. You sit there and eat these sweeties. Lizzie'll be back soon."

Toby thrust out a grubby hand for the tube. He sat in front of Abel Arthur Grey and slowly poured a multi-coloured stream of sweets into a pile in front of him. He began to put them into his mouth, one after another. Lizzie saw that already he had forgotten her.

"That's him out the way!" she thought exultantly. "Now—the witch!"

She went cautiously down the path that led by the side of the church. When she reached the corner she stopped and peered round. Her eyes went straight to the tomb of *Hannah Post of this*

16

*Parish and Albert Cyril beloved husband of the above 1802–1879
Peace Perfect Peace.*

Nothing.

"Witch!" called Lizzie softly. "Witch! Where are you?"

Silence.

"Done this before,' thought Lizzie, "pretended not to be here."

"Witch!" she called again, a little louder this time. "Witch!"

No answer. Lizzie stood and wheeled about on her shadow and raked the graveyard for a sudden snatch of tell-tale black rags. Nothing.

"P'raps she's annoyed," Lizzie thought. "P'raps she's mad at me for not coming before. Ages since I've been, it is."

"Listen, witch," she said softly, "I'm sorry I've not been lately. But there's been the school play, see, and end of term concert, and—"

She broke off. There it was! There was a rough clamour which to any casual stroller in graveyards would seem only the coarse, racketing cries of rooks. But Lizzie, who had heard the sound before, knew differently. It was laughter, the unmistakable laughter of a witch—her witch.

"Oh, witch!" she cried. "You *are* there! But where are you? I can't—"

"I spy with my little eye!" came that familiar cracked voice.

"Oooh! But I can't see you! Where are you? Please, witch?"

"Ha! Right under your nose!"

Lizzzie jumped back, and again heard the laughter, but much more faintly this time.

"Where?" she cried. "You're not going away, are you? Don't go! Come visible, witch, please!"

"Hide and seek!" crowed the witch. "Look for me, girl! Look for me!"

What began then was a mad game of hide and seek, a knee-banging unsteady running among tombstones with the grass in places nearly waist-high, and not a clue but the high cackling of the hidden witch. As Lizzie searched, part of her wanted to find

17

the witch and part of her already wished that she had never come to the graveyard at all, that she'd let well alone while she had the chance.

"Witch! Witch!" she half-screamed at last. "I'll never find you. And it isn't fair—how can I find you if you aren't *there*?"

Her answer was a cackle from where the shade was deepest and the grass longest, and Lizzie, turning hopelessly, gasped.

"Oh! You're there!" she cried, and began to thrust her way forward knee-deep and slowly, as if wading through water. As she went she kept her eyes fixed on the witch, and so she actully *saw* her disappear. First a high, malicious cackle, then a dissolving of that thin face and those twitching black rags into—nothing! She dwindled like smoke into the sunless gloom that was always under those particular yews on even the hottest summer day.

"Oooh!" Lizzie was furious now. "You cheat, you cheat!"

She stamped uselessly (for what use was a stamp that could not be seen for undergrowth?).

No answer.

"Gone!" thought Lizzie. "Sure as eggs—gone."

She stood for a moment longer and then began, very slowly, the long climb up the graveyard. She made for the path, away from the nettles. She walked with her head bent, angry at having been cheated, but even sadder because it seemed now as if she had lost her witch for ever.

"And all my own fault, I suppose," she thought.

She lifted her head then and drew in a sharp breath, because there, right in front of her, was the witch, thoroughly at home now, sitting where she had so often sat before on the tomb of the Perfectly Peaceful Posts. She went on knitting quite unconcernedly as if the game of hide and seek had never happened at all.

Lizzie took a little step forward.

"It's nice to see you again, witch," she offered—not altogether sure that she meant it, at that particular moment. The witch was even trickier than Lizzie had remembered—not so safe, more

18

likely to spring sudden spells. This was a toad-turning mood she was in, if ever there was one.

"Hmm!" sniffed the witch. "Easy enough to *say*!"

"But it is nice!" cried Lizzie. "I mean it!"

"Hmmm! Then where've you been? Eh? Answer that! Forgotten me, hadn't you? *I* know!"

"No, I hadn't, really I hadn't!" cried poor Lizzie. "I've been meaning to come the minute school broke up. And the holiday only started an hour ago, and here I am already! So I *must've* wanted to see you, mustn't I?"

"Not manners." The witch was talking to herself now. "Here one minute, gone the next! Not manners."

"*She's* a fine one to talk!" thought Lizzie incredulously.

Aloud, she said: "But I'll come every day and see you now, honest I will. Every day."

"Easy to say," returned the witch, unmollified. Then, lifting her head and looking so hard at Lizzie that she actually began to back away: "Every single day? Rain or shine? Good or ill? Hell or high water? Come what may?"

Lizzie swallowed and nodded.

"Promise?" The witch shot her head forward startlingly, and Lizzie found herself up against a tombstone.

"P-promise."

The witch sank back like a raven into its feathers.

"Hmm. Good." A finger stabbed out and Lizzie jumped. "Not saying I'll be here, mind! *I* ain't made any promises."

Dumbly Lizzie shook her head.

"Might be here—might not. Depends. But mind you are."

Lizzie nodded. She swallowed.

"Ask her," she thought, "now. . . ."

"Witch," she said carefully, "it's my Gramma's birthday today."

The witch took no notice.

"She's seventy. I've decorated her cake, with sweets and that, and candles. . . ."

Still the witch ignored her.

"And I've made her a present as well. Knitted her a tea-cosy, a yellow one, with a blue bobble."

"Hmm!" cried the witch. "Don't believe in birthdays."

"Don't you?" cried Lizzie, delighted. "Don't you really? I bet you're hundreds of years old, and I bet *you* don't get older—not *really* older, I mean. . . ."

The witch shrugged.

"Don't get birthdays," she said. "*I* don't get no tea-cosies."

"So don't you think," Lizzie was very careful now, "don't you think it'd be nice if *Gramma* didn't have any more birthdays? I mean, didn't get *older*—stopped how she is, like you do."

Again the witch shrugged.

"Up to her," she said.

"Oh but it isn't," cried Lizzie. "It's up to you! She can't *help* getting older, see, not like you can. But what if . . . what if you was to do a spell, or if you was to give her a wish. Then she could *wish* for that! Oooh, could you? It'd be like a birthday present

20

for her. . . ."

The witch, uncommunicative as ever, knitted and mumbled.

"You'd like my Gramma, if you met her," said Lizzie. "Honest, you would."

"Grammas," replied the witch briefly, "is folks' own businesses."

"Have *you* got a gramma?" Lizzie was gape-mouthed at the very thought ("*Thousands* of years old, *she'd* be!" she thought).

"If I had a gramma, she'd be my business, and if I hadn't she wouldn't," said the witch obscurely.

Lizzie tried again.

"But you *would* like my Gramma. Bit like you, she is, in a way." She had a sudden inspiration. "And . . . and she *loves* knitting—always knitting, Gram is!"

"Well I don't!" snapped the witch, and Lizzie saw that she had said the wrong thing. "Spelling's what I like. Can she?"

"Can she what? Oh, no!" said Lizzie craftily. "She isn't *half* as clever as you. That's why I thought you might give her a wish, see."

The witch preened, and Lizzie pressed her advantage.

"And—and I could knit *you* a tea-cosy as well, if you liked. You give her a birthday wish, and I'll give you—"

She broke off. The witch seemed to have stiffened, and was looking beyond Lizzie at something over her shoulder.

"What's that!" she snapped, and almost in the same instant Lizzie heard a familiar voice and froze with shock.

"Hello!"

It was Toby, saying "Hello" to the witch. (He said Hello to everyone. He'd say Hello to Jack the Ripper himself, so Patty always said.)

"Oh!" cried Lizzie, her mind a-spin with pictures of toads. "Toby!"

She turned towards him and then back again to the witch to implore her not to change Toby into a toad, and—

Gone!

"Hello," said Toby again. There was mud *and* chocolate all

over him now. He looked like some kind of mucky little cherub with his tight silver curls and blackened face. He beamed at Lizzie and she ran to him, light-headed with relief.

"Oh Toby!" She took his hand: "Just look at you!"

They began to walk together out of the graveyard. But there was one thing Lizzie had to be sure of. She stopped and knelt in front of Toby so that their eyes were on a level.

"Toby—did you see that witch?"

He looked back at her with his clear blue eyes and said nothing at all, and she was certain, absolutely certain, that he had no idea what she was talking about. He had seen—perhaps—an old lady dressed in black knitting in the graveyard. And there was nothing unusual about that.

Lizzie picked him up and whirled him round, and cried: "Come on, Toby, quick! Birthday party now, and cake! Yippee!"

They did light the candles, later, just before Gramma cut the

cake. (Not that she did not think *that* a pity. "Too good to cut, this is," she said, "by half!")

"All right," agreed Lizzie. "But you must blow as well. Hard. And wish, remember! Wish! Now—one, two, three!"

They blew, and the candles went out, every one of them, leaving a definite little darkness for a moment, like that after a firework has gone out.

"I wished," said Gramma softly, nodding to herself. "I wished. . . ."

And Lizzie was satisfied. Because after all, witch or no witch, *everyone* is entitled to a birthday wish, if they can blow out the candles.

Lizzie Dripping
and the Little Angel

Lizzie was sitting on a rug in the garden stuffing a green silk frog with rice when Aunt Blodwen came up the path. Towser got up and barked at her. He had never got used to Aunt Blodwen, or else did not want to.

"Morning, Lizzie," she said. "Keeping an eye on your brother, are you?"

Toby was digging, as usual. All you could see of him was his bottom, his heels and his white floppy sun-hat.

"I'm making this frog," said Lizzie. "Toby's all right."

"Keeping an *eye*, though, I should hope," said Aunt Blodwen. "And trying to be a help to your Mam. Supposed to save work, great girls like you, Lizzie, not make it."

Lizzie did not answer. There was never much point in holding a conversation with Aunt Blodwen. It was like being up against a high stone Welsh wall. She contented herself with thinking "Sorry for *her* kids, if she had any," and held up the finished frog. He flopped beautifully, and she could feel the rice slithering under the thin green silk that was his skin.

"Two buttons for your eyes, and you're done, frog," she told him. "Take this lot in, better, before Toby gets among it."

She gathered up the odds and ends of material, stuffed them into the scrap bag and went indoors. Patty and Blodwen were already sitting with cups of tea.

"*Smell* a cup of tea going, can Aunt Blod," thought Lizzie.

24

She put the bag on a chair and went to the mantelshelf for the button box.

"Not there, Lizzie!" cried Patty. "Up to your room, if you please! I don't know—holiday hardly started and cluttering up house already. Now do start as you mean to go on, our Lizzie, else you and me'll be falling out, I can see that."

"All right, Mam." Lizzie took the button box, picked up the scrap bag and made for the stairs.

"All the same, kids," she heard Patty say. "Though I daresay you and me was no different, Blod, in our time."

"Oh, I don't know." Blodwen's high Welsh voice floated up the stairs, as doubtless it was meant to. "Quite a help to my Mam I was, as I remember. Proper little housewife. But one of seven I was, see. Makes a difference, you know."

"Oh yes," thought Lizzie. "We all know about *that*. What's she doing round here anyway? Something's up, *I* know. . . ."

She tossed the scrap bag on her bed, took the box of buttons

25

and went and sat on the top stair. There she started rummaging for a pair of matching frog's eye buttons, and listened to what was going on down below.

". . . lovely little lad he is," she heard Aunt Blodwen say. "Proper little angel. And not a scrap of trouble, Megan says."

"I daresay you'll enjoy having him, Blod," came Patty's voice. "Be a bit of company for you, having none of your own."

"Through choice, Patty, through *choice*," Blodwen reminded her. "Told Arthur, I did, right from the start. And no *children*, Arthur, I said. Like things neat and tidy I do, and as they should be. Not all that mess and clutter children make, and the noise into the bargain. Neat and tidy and nice and quiet, that's how I like it."

"Oh, I know, Blod," agreed Patty. "You've always said. And I'm bound to say I can't see you with kids—no offence, of course."

"And none taken, Patty," came Blodwen's voice, tight and high.

26

"But you'll enjoy having this little lad a week or so—what did you say his name was?"

"Jonathan. Lovely name, Jonathan. Got a bit of class to it, that name has. And ten years old—her eldest, see. Lovely child, she says, and not a scrap of trouble from morning till night."

"*I* bet," thought Lizzie. "What's she on about? These'll do. Look good, that frog will, with yellow eyes." She shut the button box and went down.

"Our Lizzie'll help you out with him," Patty said. "Won't you, duck?"

"Won't I what?" asked Lizzie, knowing perfectly well.

"Your Auntie Blodwen's got a little nephew coming. Your Uncle Arthur's just gone to fetch him. Ten years old. John his name is."

"Jonathan, Patty," said Blodwen. "Jonathan."

"Well—near enough," said Patty cheerfully. "You can't be coming out with a mouthful like Jonathan every time you speak. Anyhow, you could help out a bit, Lizzie. Get him to know the other kids, and that."

"Aye, well . . . we shall have to see," said Aunt Blodwen. "Thank you for the tea, Patty." She got up, clutching her handbag to her. She always carried it like this, as if she were all the time afraid of being robbed.

"Thinks I'll get him into trouble," thought Lizzie. "That's what she thinks."

"We shall have to see," said Aunt Blodwen again. "Got her hands full with her own brother, I daresay."

"Oooh!" shrieked Patty. "I clean forgot! What's he up to!"

She flung open the door and there was Toby, still squatting in the border, putting stones in his tin bucket to hear them clang.

"Ah, bless him!" cried Patty fondly. "He's hardly moved this past hour. Going to be like his father, Blod, you can see that. Can't get Albert out of the garden, you know. He'd live in that greenhouse, if you'd let him."

"Gets hisself *dirty*, though, don't he, Patty?" said Aunt Blodwen dubiously. "Just look at him!

27

"Ah, bless him!" cried Patty. "Bit of dirt don't hurt, do it, my lamb? Give your Aunt Blodwen a kiss then, shall you, my pet?"

Blodwen clutched her handbag more fiercely than ever (using it as a shield now, Lizzie thought) and edged quickly past Toby and on down the path.

" 'Bye, then!" she cried. "See you soon, Patty!" and her sensible heels clacked away over the stones.

Lizzie grinned.

"That did it," she thought with satisfaction. "Good old Toby."

"I don't know. . . ." Patty was staring after Blodwen, wiping her hands on her apron, not because they needed it, but because it was a habit she had.

"Don't know what, Mam?"

"Your Aunt Blodwen. How she'll get on with that little lad. No more idea about kids than flying kites. . . . Still, not our worry, I suppose."

"Do her good," suggested Lizzie. "She don't know how the other half lives. You said that yourself, Mam."

"Why, you little . . . !" Patty laughed despite herself. "What's that you're making?"

"Frog." Lizzie held him up by his hind legs.

"Ugh!" cried Patty.

"Just going to put his eyes on," Lizzie told her. "Yellow eyes, he's going to have."

"Well, as long as you don't let Toby get hold of them." Patty was already turning back into the house. "Feel as if I've swallowed a few buttons myself, this morning."

"Don't you feel well, Mam?"

"Oh, I shall live, I daresay. Keep an eye on Toby, shall you, while I get on? Your father'll be back to dinner and I'm all behind as it is."

And so the morning passed, and Lizzie made another rice-filled frog, so pleased was she with the first. This time he was of yellow crimplene with red eyes, but he was not so froggy as the first because the rice did not slither under her fingers through the crimplene as it did through the silk.

At dinner time over the steak-and-kidney pie and peas Patty told Albert about the little angel. "Oooh, she's in for something like a surprise," she said. "I've yet to see the lad that's an angel— nor the lass either, for that matter."

"Present company excepted, of course," said Albert, and winked at Lizzie over a knifeful of peas.

"Oooh!" Patty rolled up her eyes and threw up her hands, and even Lizzie, in all honesty, was bound to say: "Not an *angel*, Dad, not me. Don't think I should like that much, anyhow."

"I should bet my last tenpence," said Patty, getting up and stacking the plates, "that he'll be round here to be from under Blod's feet before he's hardly had time to unpack his things."

"What's he coming for, then?" enquired Albert. "Give his mother a rest?"

"Well—you know," said Patty meaningfully. She lowered her

voice. "More a *family* matter, Albert. Mum going into hospital. *You* know."

Albert looked puzzled for a moment, then his face cleared. "Oh. Aye, I see."

"And so do I," thought Lizzie. "His Mum's having a baby. Why don't she say so? They never still think I think babies get found under gooseberry bushes. Toby didn't, that *is* certain."

Toby was gravely pushing peas about in the gravy swimming in the tray of his high chair.

"Gramma got her bus all right, did she?" asked Albert.

"Aye. She'll not be back until five. Likes a good rummage round shops, does Ma, though what she finds to need at her age, I don't know."

"Er—what d'ye say I take Toby with me this afternoon?" he suggested. "Give you a break."

"Oooh, I wouldn't say no," said Patty, as if Toby had been under *her* feet all morning, not Lizzie's. "Be all right, will he?"

"Putting in a new bath at the Cobbses," said Albert. "And you know her. Daft as a brush about babies, is Elsie. Give you a chance to get off and do something as well, Lizzie. What'll you do this afternoon?"

"Oooh . . ." Lizzie pulled her helping of tart towards her. "I dunno, Dad. But I'll think of something. . . ."

By the time Albert and Toby went off an hour later, Lizzie had thought of something. The house and garden were very quiet now. Patty had gone to lie down. This was something she very rarely did, and Lizzie was glad that Gramma was off in Kipton and not to know about it.

"We should only get all that stuff about sleeping on in the day, and graveyards," she thought, and immediately regretted thinking it, because the word "graveyard" to Lizzie meant only one thing.

"Did promise that old witch," she thought. "And kept it, I have, all week. And she wasn't even *there*, yesterday."

Lizzie, for once, did not want to go to the graveyard. What she wanted was to go to the lake at the bottom of Larkins' garden

30

and lie there in the rowing boat under the trees, reading.

"After all—could perhaps nip down to the graveyard after tea," she told herself, though she knew that this was not at all likely. She went to the bottom of the stairs and called up softly: "Mam! Mam!"

There was no reply. The only sound in the house was the heavy ticking of the clock, and even that seemed a drowsy, hot-summer-afternoon ticking, as if time were deliberately going more slowly than usual, the miser clock hoarding the golden hours against the winter. Lizzie looked at it, and listened. Then quite deliberately she took off her wristwatch and laid it on the table.

"Don't *want* to know what time it is," she thought. "Not this afternoon. Now what? Best leave a note, I s'pose."

She was glad that her mother was asleep. Every now and then Patty had qualms about letting Lizzie go in the boat, though she had promised never to untie it when she was there alone. She simply stepped into it, in its mooring place under the trees and lay there, reading, dreaming, dipping her hands in the cold water—savouring it with her fingers.

Lizzie wrote *Gone to Larkins* on a scrap of paper and left it on the table under the teapot. Then she took her book and a cushion and went quietly out. Towser got up and stretched and wagged his tail. Lizzie patted him.

"Can't, old chap," she told him. "You'd only jump in, or something, and chase them ducks."

At the end of Church Lane Lizzie looked out of the corner of her eye towards the graveyard, but again thought "Don't matter—always go later"—and turned left instead of right. She was still half looking the other way and so banged right into the boy. She stepped back, thought "Who's that?" and then he said:

"You Lizzie Dripping?"

Lizzie instantly collected herself. "Penelope Arbuckle, my name is," she told him.

"That's right—Lizzie Dripping. My Auntie Blod told me. Said you'd got pigtails and a turn-up nose, and you have."

"Oh—you're Jonathan," she said.

He nodded. He did look rather like an angel, Lizzie was bound to admit, with his fair hair and round face. It was not his fault, of course, that Blodwen was his aunt. This was a misfortune that might have happened to anyone, and Lizzie sympathised with it.

"I was coming to your house," he said. "She told me to. I wanted to climb the trees, but she wouldn't let me."

"No," Lizzie thought, "she wouldn't." She was sorry for him. But more than anything she wanted to be away on her own in that watery world under the willows, and so she said: "Sorry, I can't play now. Got to go somewhere, see. But I will later, honest."

"After tea?" he asked.

"Got to have my hair washed. Tomorrow. I'll see you tomorrow. *I* know some trees we could climb."

He looked at her, then at the book and the cushion. Lizzie

32

hoped that she was not turning red, because it was a kind of a fib she had just told him.

"Sorry," she said again.

He shrugged. "It's all right. I'll find something."

So Lizzie, feeling mean and small, went on down between the steep banks of Mark Lane and when she reached the bend, turned and looked back. The boy still stood there, looking after her, though he immediately turned away.

The Larkins were not at home. Mrs Larkin always went to market on Fridays and her husband was at work. Slowly Lizzie walked under the trees by the water's edge. It was cool under there, a special, delicious summer cool, all the better for the knowledge that in a single step she could be out of it again and under the hot sun. She sniffed the cold, inexplicable smells of the water and weeds and ferns and was happy to be alone there with the whole afternoon ahead of her and time something only to be forgotten.

The thought of the witch, perhaps at this very moment waiting invisibly in the graveyard for Lizzie's visit, floated to the top of her mind again and she pushed it down.

"Doesn't matter," she told herself yet again. "Go tonight, I will." And if Patty would not let her (Friday really was the night she always washed Lizzie's hair), then it would not be her fault.

"Ooooh!" Lizzie stopped dead and a little gasp flew from her lips.

For a moment, for a single moment, she had seen the witch— not the witch herself, but her reflection in the thick green water-mirror below. Lizzie whirled to look back over her shoulder.

"Couldn't have been," she told herself. "Can't have a reflection if there's nothing there to *be* reflected."

Shaking her head to emphasise the truth of this, she came to where the boat was moored and stooped to pass under the low boughs. She came to the lake's edge and there, staring up at her, was the witch in the water again!

"Oh!" Lizzie straightened and caught her hair in a branch and ducked again and lost a pigtail by its roots, or so it felt.

Lizzie crouched there, right near the damp grasses and with flies and insects drawn to her warmth like moths to candles. Was her witch a new kind of being now—a witch-in-the-water? And if so, was she still there, actually live and solid (if ever a witch can be said to be either of these things)? Was she *there*, in the sense that a mermaid is there in the sea? Or had she now become a mere reflection—because a reflection, thought Lizzie, is only really another name for a shadow. A shadow on water. The difference is that a land-shadow is only a silhouette, but a water shadow is a painting, a real portrait, with depth and colour and real stares from real eyes.

"I'll try," thought Lizzie. "See if she *is* still there—can talk."

"Witch!" she called softly. "Witch, are you there?"

There was no reply, and nor, though Lizzie stared ever so hard and long, was there the merest deep-down glimmer of a witch's shape in the quiet green water. All at once there was a flapping and squawking and Lizzie leapt to see the Larkins' ducks and moorhens thrown into a flurry on the other side of the lake.

"Not a fox," thought Lizzie, "not this time of day. A—witch?"

The birds shrugged their wings down again and gathered themselves back into their proper shapes and the place went very quiet again. Lizzie regarded the boat.

"Shall I, or not?"

An afternoon afloat in that quiet spot had become quite a different prospect with the possibility now of a witch in the willows.

"Witch!" she said loudly and abruptly, crossly even, because her pleasure was being spoilt. "Witch, if you're there, come on out!"

But the witch did not come out. And because it is difficult to feel both afraid and angry at the same time, Lizzie shrugged her shoulders, tossed her book and cushion into the boat and herself climbed carefully down after them.

Immediately the feel of the afternoon came flooding back to her and things were just as she had imagined them and wanted

them to be. She smiled and arranged her cushion and lay propped there for a while and without even opening her book. She trailed a hand in the icy water. She stared up through the swarming green and gold yet dusky air to the sky beyond the boughs, and even the whistle of birds was green and liquid. Her happiness was so real that Lizzie felt she could have wrapped it up, if she had wanted, and put it in her pocket, to keep. She felt the gentle sway of the boat and could hear all the water sounds about her, the sucks and plops and splashes that gave away the life that was happening even in that quiet pool. She stared and listened and in the end drifted, quite naturally, into a kind of dream. . . .

Lizzie woke with a start. She opened her eyes, then shut them straight away against the dazzle. She struggled upright and the boat swayed dangerously, and once she was sitting up with her eyes open again she saw at once that she was adrift. Stupidly she stared about her. The bank was far away on all sides and the sun beat down and she thought fleetingly "Like the Ancient Mariner!" Then she thought, "The witch! It *was* her, after all!"

Fearfully she scanned the undergrowth, seeing in her mind's eye how that witch must have come creeping down, stooped above Lizzie's own sleeping form and then slowly, wickedly, untied the knotted rope. . . .

"Best get ashore, anyhow," she thought. "Quick, before she sees me!"

She bent for the oars. They were not there.

"Gone!" Her hand flew to her mouth. She was properly adrift now on that tideless pool, could stay there motionless and spellbound for ever if she were not rescued.

"What'll I do? What if Mam has—? What time . . . ?" Her eyes went to the blank white mark on her wrist where her watch had been. "Oh . . . oh . . . !"

She tried to paddle then, with her hands, furiously. But all that happened was that the boat went round and round in little rocking circles and she felt the cold water flying up and soaking through her shirt.

"Can't get out," she thought, "can't *swim*. . . . Weeds, Mrs Larkin says—ooh, and a great fish with snapping teeth—a pike! Old Nick, that's what she calls it—and they've all seen it, all the Larkins. Says it's been there in the mud on the bottom for years, growing and growing, and eats all her little ducks it does, every spring. Like a kind of monster . . . have your arm off, she says. Jaws like a nutcracker. . . . Oh!"

She scanned the quiet surface of the pool for the hint of a wicked black fish and wondered fleetingly if it were not a witch fish, in league. . . . She wrapped her arms about herself and sat helpless while the boat gently swung itself into motionlessness again.

"What if Mam doesn't see my note? What if the Larkins don't get back till late? What if—what if they've gone off on their *holidays*? Could've. . . . Ooooh, and what if that fish comes up of an evening to feed, like the cows do?"

She pictured the dusk falling, the gnats hanging in low clouds over the water, the slow fade of bird-song, the evil fish coming up from his muddy bed, lurking, circling, grim jaws a-twitch.

"Ooooh!" she quavered. "I'm frit, I am!"

The golden dream was gone into nightmare now.

Then for the second time that day fear changed in a single moment to anger.

"That witch!" she thought fiercely. "Spiteful thing she is!" Then, "Witch!" she half screamed. "You come on out! D'you hear me? You come and get me off this lake this minute!"

There was no reply. The sky hung motionless in the lake. Lizzie stared. There—again—mirrored in water but invisible in air, that infuriating witch.

"Witch!" She really was screaming now. "Witch!"

The reflection sank to the bottom of the pool—or whatever reflections do when they disappear.

Lizzie was half sobbing now. She brushed a hand angrily across her eyes and looked about for help—inspiration—any-thing. And she saw, incredibly, a moving blue shape beyond a bush on the nearest bank.

"Hey!" she cried. "Help! Help!"

The bushes parted and a face peered through. It was the boy.

"Ooooh—I—it's you! Thank *goodness*! Help me, won't you? I'm stuck out here and no oars and Mam'll be missing me soon and—"

"How did you get out there then?" he asked. "Without oars?"

"Ooooh—*I* don't know! *Do* something, won't you. Please?"

Still he made no move.

"You were yelling just now," he said. "I heard you. You were yelling 'Witch!' What witch? I don't see any witch. And who believes in witches anyway? Don't tell me—"

"Shut up!" hissed Lizzie over the water. "Be *quiet*, won't you?"

She took a quick scan over the lake, fearful that reflections had ears.

"All right,' said the boy, "keep your hair on."

37

"*Do* help,' she begged. "That rope, there by the tree. It's ever so long if you untie it. You untie it, and throw it out."

He nodded and started towards the tree.

"Funny," thought Lizzie fleetingly, "not told him which tree yet, and he knows. What if . . . ? No. Why should he? Any case, I saw that witch . . . her all right!"

"Here you are—catch!" shouted Jonathan, and threw the rope. It fell a long way short.

"Tie a knot in the end," Lizzie instructed him. "A big knot. That'll make it go further."

He struggled with the wet rope and Lizzie watched and felt ashamed already of her suspicions. He threw the rope again. It fell only just short. And again. Then again. That time Lizzie caught it.

Elated, she cried, "You've done it! Oh *thanks*!"

"Pull now, shall I?"

"Let me just sit properly—wait. That's it. Now, pull."

He pulled. The boat swung smoothly into the bank. A little thud and she was as good as home and dry.

"Tie it round again, shall I?" he asked, and she nodded. She picked up her book and cushion and tossed them ashore. As she prepared to climb out herself Jonathan came and held out a hand.

"I can manage," said Lizzie. "It's all right. I'm used to it."

But he still held out his hand and she took it, or thought she did. Afterwards, she could not remember what happened except that the boat lurched under her, she threw out an arm to regain balance and next minute went into the water, headlong.

"Oooh!" she shrieked, and spray flew in a blinding mist and in it she thought she glimpsed the witch. And the water was icy and she screamed again because of the cold and the shock and the swift picture she had now of a snapping black pike with teeth like saws—Old Nick.

How she got out was a mystery, too. Jonathan seemed to be helping and yet not helping, shouting and leaping and pulling, then letting go and grabbing again. It seemed to take a very long while. Even wet to the bone as she was and spluttering, and even jumbled among visions of the state of her sandals and of Patty's face, came the thought "He's enjoying it!"

On the bank she shook herself like a wet dog. It had little effect. She felt like a waterfall.

"Home," she thought dully.

Clutching her book and cushion she began the long squelch home. Jonathan came too, but spoke only once.

"You'll catch it," he said, half-way up Mark Lane, and left her at the corner.

Numbed now by disaster, it did not surprise Lizzie to meet Gramma by the stone steps, arms full of parcels, hat awry.

"Lizzie!" she screamed. "Where you *been*?"

"F-f-fell in the lake," chattered Lizzie. "And oh Gram, Mam'll kill me!"

"You'll have the pneumonia!" shrieked Gramma. "That's what you'll have! Quick, girl!" and she gave Lizzie a push up

the steps with her black pastic shopping bag. "And what's *she* doing?"

"In b-b-bed," said Lizzie, "p-p-poorly."

"In bed!" cried Gramma. She pushed past Lizzie now and marched on ahead. "Nice thing. If that don't beat all. Lying in bed and her child half drownded! Whatever's got into her?"

She threw open the door, then turned. "You get them shoes and socks off," she ordered, "and wait."

Lizzie bent and did as she was told.

"Now get in and stand on here," ordered Gramma, reappearing. She laid a towel on the floor. Thankfully Lizzie stepped inside.

"And now off with the lot!" said Gramma. "And rub yourself with this!" She tossed in another towel and went to the foot of the stairs.

"Patty!" she called. "Patty!"

There was no reply.

"Asleep!" Gramma was disgusted. "My own flesh and blood and the way *I* brought her up. *I* don't know. I really don't know. You stop there and I'll fetch things out your drawer. No need to tell her. Only make the devil's own fuss, and a fine one to talk, I must say."

"B-b-but my hair," quavered Lizzie. "It's s-soaked."

"We'll wash it," said Gramma tersely, and began to climb the stairs with her square, flat-footed tread.

Lizzie, towelling herself in a daze, began to feel warmth and relief running together through her veins.

"Of course!" she thought. "Friday night—hair washing!"

Her glance fell on her watch, lying where she had left it.

"Almost as if I'd *known* I should fall in. . . ." she thought. "Queer . . ."

Mechanically she picked it up and held it to her ear. It was ticking sweetly.

"Dead, you'd've been, watch, if you'd've been on my wrist this afternoon," she told it. Then she pulled the towel round her and Gramma appeared with a jumper and jeans and Lizzie smiled at her and Gramma, shaking her head, actually smiled back. . . .

Lizzie Dripping
Tries a Spell

Lizzie Dripping was busy tempting fate, as usual. It did not *look* as if she were. It looked as if she were simply shredding petals from a daisy and playing the old game of "He loves me, he loves me not." But the game Lizzie was playing was far more dangerous. She was playing "witch or not".

Yesterday she had not been to the graveyard at all. Instead she had broken her promise, and fallen into Larkins' pond. Today she was not sure whether she could face the witch, and was plucking a daisy to decide for her.

"Witch—not—witch—not—witch—*not*!"

Delighted that fate had come down exactly in line with her own inclinations, Lizzie jumped up.

"That's it, then—not!"

It had not, after all, been her decision, but the daisy's. She went round into the little orchard and sat in the swing. Up she went, and the world began to seesaw, went all sloping and different. She hung back her head and gazed at the undersides of leaves and boughs and thought what mysterious things apples were, and wondered what it would be like to be a bird.

"Smashing," she thought. "Swooping about all day and sleeping in trees. Bet it's lovely in a tree at night, all rustly, like rain on your window. Wonder what it feels like, flying . . . bit like swinging, I s'pose."

She heard a hoarse caw, like that of a crow, and thought, "Not a crow, I shouldn't be, if I was a bird. Something pretty, some-

42

thing all—a swallow. Yes, that's what I'd be. A swallow."

The swing all of a sudden seemed to be soaring and swooping like a swallow, very fast and high, and again Lizzie heard that rough cry and knew in the instant that it was not a crow at all.

"The witch!" she gasped and turned her head to look and thought she glimpsed a snatch of black in the greenery and tried to slow the swing so that she could jump off.

"Turn *me* into a crow, she would, for two pins," she thought, and was even relieved to hear Aunt Blodwen's voice.

"Patty! Are you there? Patty?"

Lizzie had slowed right down now so that she had her feet on the ground again, and sat waiting.

"She'll have brought that boy," she thought. "*Said* I'd play with him today, so s'pose I'd better."

"Lizzie!" It was her mother's voice now. "Lizzie!"

"Coming!"

She went slowly through the grass and noticed three cabbage whites clinging to the warm bricks, basking. When she rounded the corner she saw Aunt Blodwen, the boy and Patty standing there looking at her.

"And what's all this I hear?" cried Patty. "All this about falling in ponds? And why wasn't I told, you sly little madam, and what about those new shoes? Where's your shoes?"

Lizzie looked at Jonathan and he looked innocently back.

"You sneak," she thought. "You *sneak*."

"I've got them on, Mam," she said, advancing a little, as if to prove that they still worked. "They're all right, honest. And I was only on the *edge*, Mam, when I fell in. Couldn't have drowned."

"Right in the middle!" cried Aunt Blodwen. "Right in the middle she was, and without oars! And to think our Jonathan might have been out there with her and heaven knows what happened. And what'd I've said to Megan, I ask you, with her little child left in my keeping, and drownded!"

"But he's not drowned," said Lizzie. Like most people whose

imaginations carry them away she was irritated when other people's did the same. Also, she wished Jonathan *were* drowned.

"You shush up!" cried Patty. "Never mind who's drownded and who ain't. Not the *point*! Times I've told you about going on that pond! You'll not go again, my lass, that's certain. And after what you'd promised, Lizzie, that's worst of it."

"I didn't row out, Mam," said Lizzie desperately. "Honest. I sat in the boat, and fell asleep, and when I woke there I was—right in the middle. *I* don't know what happened!"

All three stared at her.

"It's true, Mam!" she cried.

"Oh, very likely," cried Aunt Blodwen, "you'll be telling us next that—"

"Now what? Now what?"

It was Gramma, blinking in the strong sunlight, a little dazed and bad-tempered-looking, as if she had just woken up. Not of course that she could have—not in broad daylight.

44

Patty rounded on her.

"And *you* must have known!" she cried. "And that'll be why you washed her hair—and me thinking it was out of kindness, with me being poorly."

"Such a fuss!" snapped Gramma. "Lizzie fell into the pond and I dried her. What's to do about that?"

"And why wasn't *I* told? I am her mother, aren't I?"

"You? Snoring in bed, you was, and in broad daylight. Who'd've dried her if I hadn't've been there, I should like to know? The pneumonia, that'd've been the next thing. You can still die of it, you know. *Oh* yes, for all their clever penicillins and medicines. Woman up *our* road got took with the pneumonia last year, and *she* died of it!"

Gramma, triumphant, stood hands on hips, and Patty wilted a little and Lizzie saw that the tables had been well and truly turned. She even began to feel sorry for Patty now.

"Never mind, Mam," she said encouragingly. "I ain't got the pneumonia, I'm *sure* I ain't. I feel fine."

"Then you don't deserve to!" snapped Patty ungratefully.

"Oh well," said Aunt Blodwen, "no use crying over spilt milk, I s'pose."

"Yes," thought Lizzie, "and who *spilt* it!"

"Leave Jonathan here a bit then, shall I, while I get on?" she went on brightly. "Flowers to do, see, for chapel. My week, this week."

"Up to you, Blodwen." Patty gave a bitter laugh. "Don't go leaving him here if you think he'll end up drownded."

"Oh!" Blodwen forced a gay laugh. "Won't do that, will he? And Lizzie'll have learned her lesson now, I daresay. Wouldn't've mentioned it to you otherwise, see. Only reason was I thought it was my duty. 'If you don't tell Patty, Blodwen,' I says to myself, 'and that poor child gets herself drownded, you'll never forgive yourself.' So I tell you, see."

"Hmmm." Patty seemed no more convinced of Aunt Blodwen's good intentions than Lizzie herself was. "Well—it's up to you, I s'pose. I shall have to get on. Work to be done, even if you are fit to drop."

She turned and went in, shooting a sideways look at Gramma as she went. There was an uncomfortable pause.

"Oh well—that's fine, then, isn't it?" said Aunt Blodwen, still being bright. "You stop here, Jonathan, and play with Lizzie for a bit. Dinner at one sharp, mind, and don't get yourself dirty."

She went a few paces down the path, then turned.

"And no *trees*, Jonathan," she said. "No broken necks, not in my house, thank you."

All three watched her go down the path, off to go round people's gardens snipping flowers with her sharp Welsh scissors.

"*There* goes one that'll never fall in a pond," remarked Gramma.

Lizzie looked sideways at Jonathan's expressionless face.

"He never thinks I'm playing with *him*," she thought. "Not *now*."

"That woman," she heard Gramma's voice, "always puts me in mind of a toothbrush."

"A—who? Aunt Blodwen?"

"A scrubby little toothbrush," nodded Gramma. "Busy-bodying about."

"Oh Gramma, you are daft!" Lizzie giggled. "Makes you want to bare your teeth, you mean—like this?"

Lizzie bared them with relish.

"Don't know what I mean," said Gramma enigmatically. "Just does, that's all. No more than that. No whys or where-fores."

With that she lost interest and turned to follow Patty indoors. She paused. Her hand went to her pinafore pocket.

"Mint imperial?"

Lizzie nodded and took one, and Gramma went in.

"She never gave me one!" said Jonathan, astonished.

"I don't expect," Lizzie told him, "she wanted to."

"But you always offer round!" He was thoroughly astounded

as if a law of nature had been reversed—fish started flying or owls hooting at noon.

"Why?" asked Lizzie.

Jonathan was temporarily floored.

"Well—you just do," he said lamely at last. "It's manners."

"Oh, *them*," said Lizzie. "Well, I only give sweets to them I like, and I expect Gramma's the same. I don't think she noticed you, as a matter of fact."

She turned on her heel and went back to the green comfort of the orchard, in the hope of salvaging what was left of the morning. She sat on the swing and immediately saw Jonathan peer from behind the corner of the cottage. Pretending not to notice, she lay back as far as she could, looking upwards again, scanning the boughs for unborn apples.

"Drat him!" she thought, finding that she could not think

while she was being watched. "Why doesn't he go away?"

He did not go away.

"Wish *I* could spell," she thought. "*I'd* spell him!"

Suddenly she stretched out her whole body, seized by an idea, an idea so terrifying and awesome and yet so glorious that she could not imagine why she had not thought of it before. She flew like an arrow now, stiff with excitement.

"What if she could *teach* me! I reckon *I* could be a sort of a witch! P'raps I am, already. After all, nobody sees her, except me. Don't think so, anyhow. I bet that's it! I bet it's because I'm a bit of a witch myself. I know, I'll test it out. I'll shut my eyes, and spell that witch to be . . . to be in Farmer Stokes's hayfield. Then I'll go and look, and if she *is* there, I'll *know* I'm a witch! And then I'll ask her—ask her about spelling!"

"Can I have a go?"

Lizzie sat up. He was right by her now. She stood up.

"You can have a go," she said with extreme sweetness. "You can have a go all morning. It's all yours."

"Where're you going?" He caught up with her. "Can I come?"

"Nowhere," said Lizzie.

"What're you going to do, then?"

"Nothing."

"You said we could climb trees."

"That," she told him, "was before somebody went telling tales."

"She asked me where I'd been, so I told her."

"Yes. *And* you knew she'd come straight round telling. Spying old busybody!"

"You shut up about my Aunt Blodwen!"

"Oooh—Auntie Blodwen's little boy, are you now? You go away and play like a good boy, and mind you keep yourself clean. No climbing trees, mind!"

"And your Gramma's a rude old woman, saying she's like a toothbrush and then not handing round sweets!"

Lizzie laughed then with pure delight.

"Hee—a toothbrush! She is rude, my Gram. We're all rude at

48

our house. You keep away and you'll be all right."

She started to go in earnest now, leaving him behind.

"What *are* you going to do?" he shouted after her.

"I told you!" she called over her shoulder. "Nothing!"

"That's all there is to do round here!" he shouted after her. "Nothing! Horrible place this is. Boring rotten little place! Glad I don't live here!"

Lizzie turned for the last time.

"And so am I," she told him. "So *that's* lucky, ain't it? Come on, Towser!"

Now she really did go off, down the garden path and into Church Lane, and as she went she heard his voice after her:

"Lizzie Dripping, Lizzie Dripping,
Don't look now, your fibs are slipping!"

"Didn't take him long to learn *that*!" she thought furiously and began to run, not because she wanted to get out of earshot of the chanting (she had heard that a thousand times before) but because she felt certain that he would try to follow her, as he had done yesterday.

She slipped inside the open gate of the hayfield and flopped breathless behind the hedge. Towser did the same. There, Lizzie lay doing nothing at first but draw in the smell in gulps, the smell of new-mown hay, freshly turned and giving off its heady scents under the hot sun. It smelt like a fresh grass tastes when you chew it. Lizzie picked a lush stalk of grass from the shadow of the hedge and bit into it and the sudden sweetness burned her tongue. She sat up, all at once alert.

"What's that?"

She crouched behind the hedge and looked through. Jonathan was coming, stamping his feet as he came and chanting in time: "Auntie Blodwen's a scrubby old toothbrush, Auntie Blodwen's a scrubby old toothbrush . . ."

Lizzie clapped a hand to her mouth to smother her laughter. He was level with her now, only a few feet away through the hedge.

"Auntie Blodwen's a scrubby old toothbrush

And Lizzie Dripping's *worse*!"

He stamped his foot hardest of all on the last syllable and Lizzie's mirth gave way at once to fury.

"Lizzie Dripping's *worse*!

Lizzie Dripping's *worse*!"

"Where's he going?" Lizzie wondered. "Looking for a tree to climb, I'll bet! He'll catch it! Hope he does, and all!"

She sat back on her heels then and remembered why she was there.

"Don't seem to be here, that witch," she thought. "Could be hiding, of course. Say something out loud, I'd better. Say it something like a sort of spell. Let's think . . ."

She sat cross-legged then and drew herself up very straight backed and shut her eyes tight.

"Witch appear, witch appear!

I make you witch, out of the air!"

It came so easily that she surprised herself. So much like a

real spell did it seem that when she opened her eyes she was certain the witch would be there. Not a blink or snatch of black in sight. She let out a long sigh of disappointment. Her eye fell on a daisy.

"See what the daisy says. Sort of spell, that is."

She held the daisy in her left hand and began to nip off its petals one by one with her right.

"Witch—not—witch—not—witch—not—witch—!"

Lizzie sprang to her feet. As she did so the skylark's song went out like a candle flame and instead she heard a familiar cracked voice:

"Toad—not—toad—not—"

It was the witch, enthroned on hay, plucking a daisy with those long white fingers. Lizzie blinked. It was like seeing the witch for the first time, seeing her black cloak spread on spiking hay, her whole impossible person in so wide and sunlit a place.

"It worked!" she thought incredulously. "She's here!"

"Toad—not—toad—not—toad—*not*!"

The last fierce syllable shot Lizzie to attention.

"Pity," said the witch, and tossed the bald daisy into the air.

"Oh witch!" cried Lizzie then. "I spelled you here, and here you are!"

The witch smiled, not a real smile, at Lizzie, but her usual one, to herself.

"Hgh!" she cried. "And where were you yesterday? Eh? Eh?"

Lizzie stared back at her.

"But you know!" she thought. "You were there! It was you as—"

"I was *there*!" cried the witch, as if reading Lizzie's thought. "I know, I saw. . . ."

"But I was coming to see you later," cried Lizzie, "and I would've, really I would, if you hadn't've—"

She broke off. She did not dare accuse a witch.

"What?" The witch leaned a little nearer. "What?" she prompted. The word was a hoarse whisper.

"You—" Lizzie gulped—"you know—undid the rope, and—and made me fall in!"

The witch gathered herself then. She drew in her robes, she stretched and straightened.

"I—did—what?"

Lizzie flinched from the last spat syllable.

"Y—you were there! I saw you!"

The witch looked at her then, long and hard.

"Wherever you see me, there I am," she said musingly, half to herself. "Which is witch, you or me?"

"There you are!" cried Lizzie. "*You've* noticed, as well! That's what I wanted to see you about. You see, I think—well, I know it sounds daft, but I think *I* might be a little bit of a witch, myself . . ."

"You. . . ." murmured the witch.

"And what I *really* wondered," went on Lizzie, "was whether you could teach me to do a bit of spelling."

The witch said nothing.

"It came to me, all of a sudden," she went on. "Best idea I've

ever had in my whole life. Think, to spell!"

"Hmmm. Think it easy, do ye?" cried the witch.

"Oh no!" cried Lizzie hastily. "Oh no, witch, I don't think that! It's just that—ooh, if you could spell, you could do anything you wanted in the whole world! Like fly, for instance—fly like a bird—turn yourself *into* a bird, for that matter."

"I'm bird, times," crooned the witch. "I'm bird I'm cat I'm toad I'm shadow-in-the-water. A rare slippery one I am."

"Oh you are!" agreed Lizzie. "And I know I could never be as good at spells as you are. But if you could tell me just one, just *one* for me to try. . . ."

The witch gazed at her for what seemed a very long while and Lizzie crossed her fingers and hoped that she was not thinking dangerously.

"*I* know what it is you want," the witch announced at last. "You come a little closer, and I'll whisper."

"You will?" Lizzie could hardly believe it. "Oh *thank* you, witch!"

And she went forward and was suddenly right close up against the witch, within inches of that supernatural flesh, that elusive huddle of black rags. The whisper came. Lizzie nodded. The witch whispered again and Lizzie stepped back, dazed.

"Oh!" she exclaimed softly. "I've a spell to do! I'll do it—right away I will!"

"Wait!" snapped the witch. "Not so fast, my girl. There's reckonings to be made yet. You made a promise."

Lizzie nodded.

"Them that break promises," said the witch softly, "pay forfeits."

Lizzie's eyes widened.

"Forfeit?" she repeated at last in a small voice.

"Break a promise, pay a forfeit," nodded the witch, almost happy now. "And me to choose. *I* choose the forfeit!"

"Oh dear, oh dear!" Lizzie felt herself once again to be on the very brink of toadhood.

"Let's see," murmured the witch, "what shall it be . . . ?"

"Quick! Think of something yourself, Lizzie, before she does!" then, out loud,

"Climb the chestnut by the Adamses—*that's* hard! Break your neck doing that, Mam says."

The witch nodded slowly.

"Climb the chestnut and bring me back a green spray from the seventh bough. A green spray, for working spells."

"Long way up, *that* is," said Lizzie, "seventh bough."

"Or shall I think of something else?"

The witch, black and solitary in that wide golden landscape, was an inescapable fact, forcing Lizzie to decision.

"I—I will, then," she gulped. "I'll fetch it."

The witch, satisfied, sank back and rocked herself on the gently creaking hay. She surveyed Lizzie, considered her.

"Tricksy, you are," she murmured. "And you break promises. You bring that bough to me. Bring it tonight. You hear?"

"I—hear. In the graveyard?"

54

"Dusk. Owl-light. Come at dusk. And mark this!"

A crooked white finger stabbed and Lizzie waited. "Them that break two promises," said the witch softly, "pay two forfeits. And there'd have to be spells. I should have to do some spelling, if two promises were broken."

"Oh, I'll come!" cried Lizzie. "I will, honest! But don't—"

The witch went melting into hay. Witch—black mist—hay. Gone. The skylark throbbed and spun a long way up and all Lizzie had for comfort was the heat, the sun burning companionably into her skin. She shivered a little as she went through the gate and into the lane and walked like a sleepwalker down towards the Adamses. After a time she felt better, and remembered the spell. She said it inside her head, savouring it, and smiled.

"To think! A witch!" The thought was irresistible. "To fly at night like an owl! Go invisible on people's heels, to stop clocks ticking! Yes—*that's* the first thing I'd do—stop clocks! It'd be summer then, all year round, and Gramma'd never grow old, not ever. And flowers—them buttercups there, for instance—they'd stop open, for ever and ever. Oooh—the things I'll do if I do turn out to be a witch!"

"Lizzie!"

She came to all at once.

"Lizzie? Thought you was playing with Jonathan. Where's Jonathan?"

I don't know, Aunt Blodwen," said Lizzie innocently. "Said he wanted to climb trees—wanted me to show him some. But I wouldn't."

"Trees!" cried Aunt Blodwen. "I should think not, indeed! Better not let me catch him climbing trees!"

"Not used to it, he isn't," said Lizzie. "Break his neck, I should think—bound to."

"Oh!" shrieked Aunt Blodwen.

"His leg, anyhow," went on Lizzie. "If he didn't break his neck he'd break his leg. Or arm. Or something. Bound to."

"And tear his trousers into the bargain, I shouldn't wonder!"

cried Aunt Blodwen. "After all that was said to him. Won't I tan his backside!"

"Didn't say he *had* gone climbing, Aunt Blodwen," said Lizzie. "Just thought he might've. Don't suppose he would, really—I mean, little angel like he's meant to be. And you told him not to."

"You go and look for him, Lizzie," said Aunt Blodwen. "You go this minute!"

"Oh I can't!" said Lizzie. "I'm on a—I'm on an errand. Doing an errand for an old lady."

The witch was, after all, old, if not entirely a lady.

"Oh. Oh. Well, then, you keep a *look* out for him, Lizzie Dripping," said Aunt Blodwen. "And if you see him, just you tell him that his Aunt Blodwen wants him this minute. *I'll* give him climbing trees."

"I'll tell him," promised Lizzie, and off she went again.

"Another thing I could do if I was a witch," she thought. "Get Aunt Blodwen spelled into something and out the way. Spider, she'd make. Yes, that's it, a spider. Spider in the bath, and wash her down the plughole!"

She laughed aloud at the thought and ran the rest of the way to the Adamses. Her gaze went straight to the great chestnut whose seventh bough she was to pluck as forfeit.

"Do the forfeit first, better," she thought, "and then the spell. Just you wait, mister sneaky Jonathan, *I'll* spell you, in a bit!"

She advanced towards the tree.

"Lizzie! Lizzie!"

The voice was coming from the tree. "Well!" thought Lizzie. "He *is* up a tree! I *am* a witch, I'm *sure* I am!"

"You'd better come on down out of there!" she called up. "Your Aunt Blodwen's looking for you. Going to tan the backside of you, she says."

"I can't!" came the voice, muffled by leaves. "I'm stuck!"

"He's *stuck*!" Now Lizzie really could not believe it. "I haven't even *said* the spell yet, only practised it, inside my head. And he's stuck! Oooh—I *am* a witch!"

"Can you get a ladder?" came the voice.

It suddenly struck Lizzie as comical, this talking tree, and what with that and the staggering proof of her own witchhood, she laughed out loud.

"Can't!" she said. "Adamses are out. Don't you like it up there? Where are you?"

She went closer and looked right up through the layering boughs and could see Jonathan's face, white and boggle-eyed, in among the leaves like some rare bird.

"Not scared, are you?" she asked.

"No! No, course not. I just want to get down, that's all."

"I'll tell you what," said Lizzie thoughtfully. "I'll run and fetch your Aunt Blodwen. *She'll* think of something."

"No! Oh no—don't! Please!"

Lizzie sat down then, where Jonathan could see her.

"P'raps—p'raps you could come up and help," came the

voice. "You're good at climbing trees."

"Oh, I am," agreed Lizzie.

"Got to go up, anyhow," she thought, "to fetch that forfeit."

Her eyes fell on a daisy, and she stretched out for it.

"Tell you what," she said, "I'll ask this daisy. See what it says."

"Ask a *daisy*?"

For answer Lizzie began to nip off the petals one by one.

"Tree—not—tree—not—tree—"

"Are you barmy, or something?"

Lizzie paid no attention.

"Tree—not—tree!"

She shrugged and got to her feet.

"I'm coming," she said.

Lizzie had climbed the chestnut tree before, though never higher than the third fork, where she had found she could actually lie along the bough, her back resting against the trunk, and fancy herself a bird, or just dream. When she reached this point, she looked up.

"Four, five, six, seven," she counted. "Nearly at the *top* that looks!"

Jonathan himself seemed to be on the next bough up, the fourth. Next minute she was on a level with him. A few inches higher, and she would be able to reach the seventh bough. She heaved herself up.

"Hey!" cried Jonathan. "Where are you going?"

"Got it!" Triumphantly she let herself down again, a spray from the magical seventh bough clutched in her hand.

"Phew!" She had no pocket, so she put the twig between her teeth.

"What on earth?"

"Now—down!"

She hung on with her hands and lowered the rest of her body carefully. Her toes sought a foothold and failed. Her feet hung in space.

"Help!"

She felt a hand clutching at the back of her shirt, and next

moment was up on a level with Jonathan again.

"See," he said. "You can't get down. Get up all right, but not down."

"Move over, can you," said Lizzie. Then there they were, both sitting side by side, "Like a pair of love birds," she thought, and giggled.

"Not funny," Jonathan said. "Hours we could be stuck up here."

"One thing," said Lizzie. "I'll not get into trouble. Only came up to help you."

"So what did you go on further up for then?" he demanded. "And what's that twig for?"

Lizzie eyed him.

"Do you believe in witches?"

"Witches?" His voice was incredulous.

"Well, do you?"

"Course not."

Lizzie looked sideways at him, hunched on his bough, thoroughly miserable and headed for certain doom, and was almost sorry for him.

"Your Aunt Blodwen'll murder you." She spoke her thoughts out loud.

"If we ever get down," he said gloomily.

"Could be up here all night if no one comes!" Now it was Lizzie's turn to be alarmed. She began to wish that she had kept her spells to herself. This particular spell seemed to have rebounded in a very unwitchlike way.

"My bottom hurts," Jonathan said. "Ages I've been up here."

"Not torn your *trousers*, I hope?" enquired Lizzie.

For answer Jonathan stretched out a leg bare almost to the knee, the trouser falling away from the seam.

"Crikey!" she exclaimed. "You did!"

There was silence then.

"Serves me right, I s'pose," Lizzie thought. "Got what I asked for, all right. Kept on about being a bird, and now I'm stuck up a *tree* like a blessed bird. Nothing to write home about, either."

"I wonder how long it *will* be," came Jonathan's voice. "Before someone finds us, I mean. I s'pose your dog wouldn't go and fetch someone?"

Lizzie shook her head. She could see Towser, head on paws away down below, oblivious and content.

"Might go home when he's *hungry*," she said. Then, "Let's play something. That's what miners do, trapped in a pit. To keep spirits up, see, and pass time. Let's play a guessing game, or something."

"I spy?" suggested Jonathan.

Lizzie heard a voice inside her head, the witch's voice. "I spy with my little eye!"

"Shall we?"

"Oh—oh! Yes. All right," she agreed.

"I spy with my little eye," began Jonathan, "something beginning with . . . g . . ."

60

An hour later they were still playing, and were beginning to run out of ideas. There was not very much to see from where they sat.

"I spy with my little eye, something beginning with . . . h. . ." said Jonathan.

"Hungry," said Lizzie instantly. "And I am. Ravenous. Dinner time, near. Mam'll go mad. And sausages, it was."

"Bet Aunt Blodwen won't give me anything," said Jonathan glumly. "Not even if we do get down, I mean."

"Never mind," Lizzie told him encouragingly. "I could bring you a few bits, out pantry. Come to our house, you could, and then Gram'd mend your trousers for you."

"I wish I'd never pushed you in pond," Jonathan said.

"You—what?" Lizzie turned on the bough to face him. "*You*?" Jonathan stared back.

"But you knew!" he cried. "You must've! Who else could it've been?"

"But I thought it was the w—" Lizzie's voice died away. "It was a rotten mean thing to do," she said.

"I know. I'm sorry, really I am."

"Listen!" hissed Lizzie, clutching at his arm.

Footsteps. Whistling.

"Help!" they both shrieked together. "Help!"

The footsteps and the whistling stopped.

"Up here!" cried Lizzie. "Up in the tree!"

"Well, if it ain't our Lizzie!" came a voice, and Lizzie really did shriek then.

"Dad! Dad! Quick. We're stuck up tree!"

Next minute Albert's face was staring up at them through the boughs.

"Eh, well," he said. "Stuck, are you?"

We've been up here hours, Dad," cried Lizzie. "Get us down, can't you? It's near dinner time!"

Albert was nodding.

"Came to do guttering for Mrs Adams," he said. "Got ladder in back," and disappeared.

"Oooh!" breathed Lizzie. "Thank heaven!"

"And leave spells alone, I'd better," she thought. "Bounced back on *me*, that one did."

Then Albert was there again, and she cried, "I spy with my little eye, something beginning with—l! And bags first down it!"

And she was, down the ladder and coming out of the tree, not in a flutter of wings like the bird she had longed to be, but one foot after another like the Lizzie Dripping she really was.